# WHERE THE GREAT BEAR WATCHES

**WRITTEN BY**

## James Sage

**ILLUSTRATED BY**

## Lisa Flather

London

AT sea in my little boat,

I am alone but not afraid.

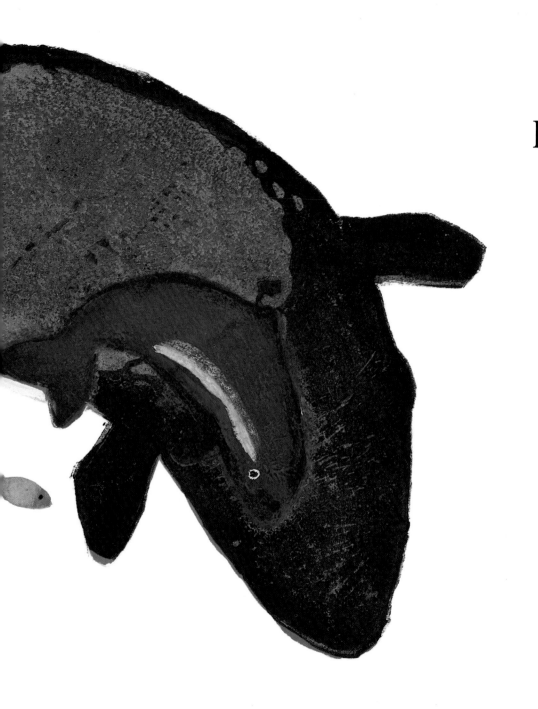

Below me swim
my friends, the fish
and the porpoise and
the whales who
haunt the deep.

Nearby are the walrus
and the seals, who give me
food, tools, clothing,
light and warmth.

Above me circle the
seabirds, wings
against the blue,
crying,
        crying,
                always crying.
And above them,
higher still, float the
peaceful clouds of dawn.

Out there, somewhere,

stalks the great bear.

"Hello, hello, great bear!" I call.

"I cannot see you, but I know you are there."

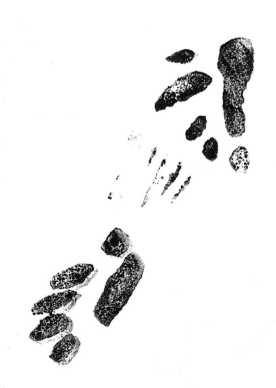

"I am your old enemy, remember?

But now I will be your friend.

I will not hurt you. And

you must promise

not to hurt me."

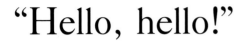

"Hello, hello!"

I call again. But it is not
the great white bear who answers.
It is the gentle wind of morning
blowing seaward from the shore.

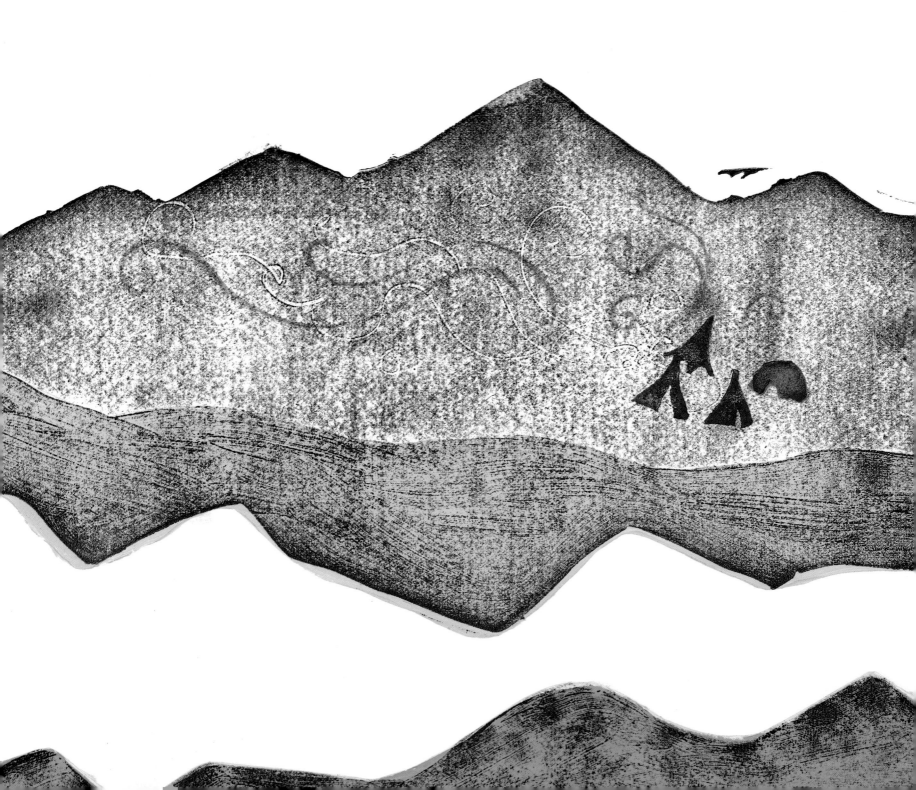

From the shore

where my brothers and sister

wait for my return.

I must help feed them.

I must feed my sled dogs, too.

I must protect them all.

I must be strong and brave, as I hunt

for food on this dark and silent sea.

For a little while, I will drift with the current. . . .
Oh, if only I could always be at sea and watch
the friendly morning sun spread light across the
water, and feel the first breeze touch my cheeks,
and taste the salt spray on my lips!

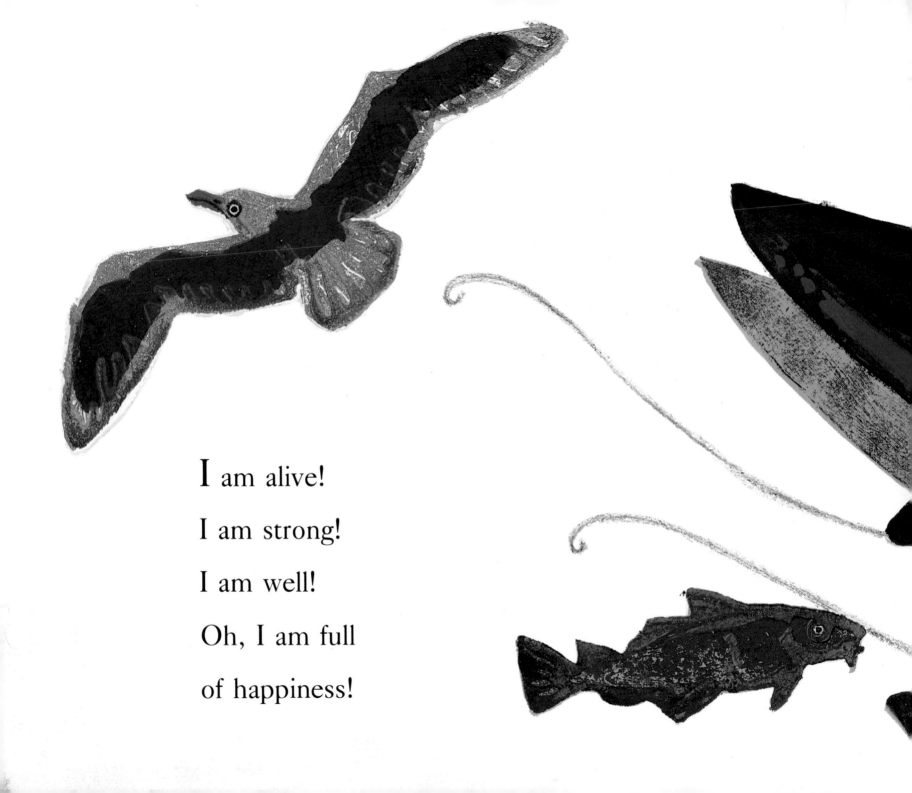

I am alive!

I am strong!

I am well!

Oh, I am full

of happiness!